# My First Kafka
## Runaways, Rodents & Giant Bugs

Retold by
**Matthue Roth**
Illustrated by
**Rohan Daniel Eason**

My First Kafka: Runaways, Rodents & Giant Bugs

Copyright text © 2013 Matthue Roth
Copyright illustrations © 2013 Rohan Daniel Eason

ISBN 13: 978-1-935548-25-6

First published hardcover edition by One Peace Books, Inc. in 2013

4 5 6 7 8 9 10

Cover and Interior Design by Richard Rodriguez
Edited by Robert McGuire

One Peace Books
43-32 22nd Street #204 Long Island City, NY 11101 USA
www.onepeacebooks.com

Printed in Korea

# Excursion into the Mountains

"I don't know!"
I cried without being heard.

"I do not know."

If nobody comes,
then nobody comes.

I've done nobody any harm.
Nobody's done me any harm.
But nobody will help me.

A pack of nobodies
would be rather fine,
on the other hand.

I'd love to go on a trip
– why not? –
with a pack of nobodies.

Into the mountains, of course.
Where else?

How these nobodies jostle each other,
their arms linked together,
these numberless feet
treading so close!

We travel so happily.
The wind blows through us
and through the gaps
in our company.

Our throats swell
and are free
in the mountains!

It's a wonder that
we don't burst into song.

# The Metamorphosis

## Part 1

Gregor Samsa always had bad dreams.
One morning he awoke to find
he'd become a giant bug.

He raised his head and saw
it was no dream.
He had a shiny brown stomach and
several little legs.

"Gregor!" his mother called.
"Are you sick?"
Gregor looked at the clock.
He saw that he had slept late.

"I'll be ready right away," he said.
"I must get out of bed
and go to my office.
I need to work today."

Gregor tried to leave his bed.
It was harder than he thought
to move all his small legs
at once.

If he moved one,
all the others
wanted to move as well.

The doorbell rang.

Gregor got so excited
that he threw himself on the floor
with a large BANG.

"Something has fallen in there!"
said the manager.

Nobody else said anything.

Gregor listened.
His sister sat at the door
and cried.

"Gregor," said his father,
"the manager is here."

"What is the matter?" the manager said.
"I demand to know!
I thought you were so calm,
and now you are in a weird mood.
Open the door now."

"I'm opening the door!" said Gregor.
"Don't give my parents a hard time!
I will go to the office
right away."

He moved against a chest of drawers
so that he could unlock the door.

Outside the door
everybody was quite puzzled.

"Did you understand a single word?"
said the manager.
"That sounded like an animal's voice."

"Perhaps he's very ill,"
said Gregor's mother.

"You must go to the doctor!"
said his sister.

Gregor realized
that nobody understood him.
He fell against the door
and turned the key
with his mouth.

Gregor leaned out
so only half his body could be seen.

His sister looked at their parents.
His mother looked at his father.
The manager looked at him.

"Now," said Gregor,
"I'll get dressed right away.
I know I'm in a fix
but I will work hard
to get out of it."

Then he lost his balance
and tripped over his many legs.

His manager ran out the front door
without turning around.

Then his father picked up a cane
and swatted at him.

Gregor tried to say he was sorry
but he couldn't say a thing.
Between blows, Gregor wriggled
back to his room.

# Part 2

Gregor woke up
in the evening.
He smelled something to eat.

By the door
sat a bowl of sweet milk.
Pieces of bread
floated inside.
Gregor almost laughed with joy.
His sister knew that milk
was his favorite drink.
Surely she had left it for him.

But he could not drink it.
Gregor no longer liked milk.
He crept back
to the middle of the room.

In the morning, Gregor's sister
opened the door
to his bedroom.
She looked inside eagerly.

She slammed the door in surprise
but then tiptoed in
and took out the milk.

She brought him fresh vegetables,
rotten vegetables,
bones from the meal last night,
some moldy cheese,
a slice of dry bread,
and a slice of bread and butter.
She left very quickly.

Gregor's small legs buzzed.
The time for eating had come.

He ate the cheese,
the moldy vegetables,
and the bones.

The fresh food
didn't taste good.
He couldn't bear
the smell.

Gregor's sister
brought him food every day,
while everyone else
was asleep.
She cleaned up after him too.

During the day
Gregor crawled back and forth
along the walls
and the ceiling.

He especially liked
hanging from the ceiling.
It was easier to breathe
up there.

But when his sister came in
Gregor always hid
under the couch.

Gregor's parents were happy about
his sister's work
but they never visited him.
One day, his mother decided
to help.

Gregor's mother and sister moved around
the furniture in his bedroom.
Gregor scuttled outside
and hung himself in the hall.
Then they left the room and
his mother glanced at Gregor.

"Gregor!" she cried.
She fell onto the couch
and lay there.

Gregor's sister heard a bell.
Their father was home.

"Mother fainted,"
said Gregor's sister.
"Gregor is out
of his room."

"I expected that," said the father.
He yelled as soon
as he saw Gregor.
He sounded both angry
and pleased.

The father filled his pockets
from the fruit bowl
and threw apple
after apple
at Gregor.

One hit his back
and fell off.

Another dove into
Gregor's back very hard.
The apple felt like it
had been nailed there.

His mother woke up.
She ran to his father
and begged him
to stop.

# Part 3

Three strange men with long beards
moved in
with Gregor's family.

They ate supper at the table
while Gregor's family
ate in the kitchen.

One night after supper,
Gregor's sister
went into her room
to play the violin.

"Do you like the music?"
asked Gregor's father.
"She can stop playing."

"Of course not!"
said the men.
"Come in here,
where it's warm and happy."

The father carried the music stand.
The mother carried the music.
Gregor's sister carried the violin.

The men listened to her play.
The father and mother
stood behind her
and watched.

Even Gregor
stuck his head
into the room.

The men started to talk again.
Gregor hoped she would
never stop playing.
It was beautiful.

The sister grew tired.
She put the violin down
and stopped playing.

"Mr. Samsa!" said the men.

Without another word
        they pointed
            their fingers...

Gregor's father told them
to leave the room.

"Most certainly!"
said the bearded men.
"We are moving out!"

Gregor lay still.
He was very hungry.

"If only he understood us,"
said the father.

"If only he understood us,"
said the mother.

"He's starting up again!"
said the sister.

But Gregor wasn't
starting up again.
He was only trying
to turn around
to go back
to his room.

Inside the bedroom
Gregor felt
he could no longer move
at all.

It was a nice feeling.

He thought of his family
and felt happy.

His head sank down
and he watched the dawn.

In the morning
they discovered
that Gregor could not move.

"Look how thin he was,"
said Gregor's sister.
"He hadn't eaten
in so long."

The three of them
left the house together
(something they hadn't done
for months)

and took the train
to a park
outside the city.

The parents decided to move
to a new apartment.
They decided their daughter
was growing
into a beautiful
young woman.

When she stepped off
the train car
and into the warm sunshine
it was like their dreams
were coming true.

# Josefine the Singer
# or, The Mouse People

## josefine

Our singer's name is Josefine. If you haven't heard her sing, you don't
know the power of a song. None of us are music lovers. Is it really a song
at all? Might it just be a kind of whistling? We all whistle, while we work,
without noticing that we are whistling.

But Josefine does not think there is any connection between her art and
whistling. To her it is special. She stands there and throws her head
back. Her mouth half-open, looking upward.

She does this anywhere. She is going to sing. The news spreads fast.
Hundreds of us come running.

## us

Our life is hard. We work all day, and we worry. Every day brings new surprises and terrors. We listen to Josefine even in emergencies. We are happy to come and just as happy to leave when she is done.

She sings best during the most dangerous times. When it is hardest for us all to come watch her. She stands there and waits for us to show up.

## safe

We protect Josefine from the outside world. But Josefine thinks that she protects us from the world with her singing. Why else do we all come to hear her, even in moments of danger? Perhaps our enemies can hear her singing.

But we still come to watch her. Her singing does not save us. It does not give us strength. But we like to come together, to huddle close and listen to Josefine.

# gone

The other day, Josefine hurt her foot at work. It was hard for her to stand up to sing. She can only sing when she stands up.

She said that she was tired. She was not in the mood to sing. We begged her, and she tried to sing. But then she shook her head. She could not.

That was yesterday. Today, she is gone. She disappeared at the time she was supposed to sing. And now we cannot find her.

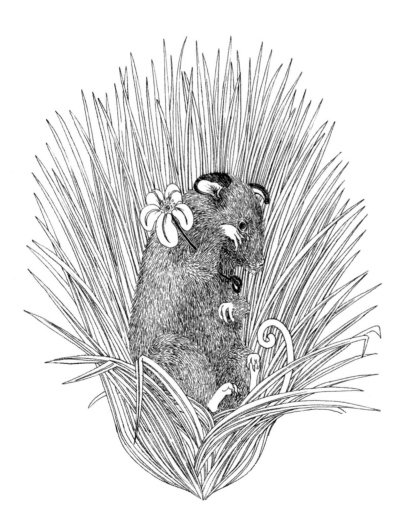